THE SECRETS OF DROON

— TONY ABBOTT —

Queen of Shadowthorn

Illustrated by David Merrell
Cover illustration by Tim Jessell

A
LITTLE APPLE
PAPERBACK

SCHOLASTIC INC.
New York Toronto London Auckland Sydney
Mexico City New Delhi Hong Kong Buenos Aires

For my brother

For more information about the continuing saga of Droon,
please visit Tony Abbott's website at
www.tonyabbottbooks.com

ISBN-13: 978-0-439-90252-6
ISBN-10: 0-439-90252-5

12 11 10 9 8 7 6 5 4   11 12/0

Printed in the U.S.A.
First printing, October 2007

Contents

One

Eric, Plain and . . . What?

Even before he crossed the street, Eric Hinkle could see his friends Neal and Julie waving at him excitedly from the library steps.

As the town librarian, Neal's mother, Mrs. Kroger, had asked the children to help with the grand opening of the library's rare books room.

"Hurry up, Eric!" said Julie. "We've got news!"

"I can just guess," Eric grumbled to himself, looking each way before stepping into the road. "I bet they both dreamed about Droon, and we'll go there, and everyone will know what happened to me."

Droon was the magical world Eric and his friends had discovered under his basement one day. It was a land of great friends like Princess Keeah and Galen the wizard. It was also a place of dangerous enemies like the bull-headed beast, Emperor Ko, and his second-in-command, the moon dragon, Gethwing.

Before they discovered Droon, Eric, Neal, and Julie were ordinary, normal kids like their friends. But since finding the rainbow stairs in Eric's basement, they had developed powerful magical abilities.

Julie could fly like a bird and change her shape whenever she wanted.

Neal had become a famous time-traveling genie named Zabilac.

Eric himself had been swiftly becoming a full-fledged wizard with many magical powers. He had dreams about Droon, saw visions, understood all sorts of old languages, and cast complicated spells. He had hoped to be as great as Galen himself one day.

Except . . .

Except that on their last visit to Droon, Eric had lost his powers. *Lost* them. All of them.

In order to defeat a powerful foe, as well as to help his friends and save Droon, Eric had used the magical staff of thorns that belonged to the mysterious Princess Salamandra.

Eric knew Salamandra was a thief of magic. She came originally from an ancient empire called Shadowthorn and traveled to different times and places through her magnificent Portal of Ages. When she told Eric that there would be a price to pay for using her staff, it didn't matter. He had to save his friends, and that's all there was to it.

But the moment he did, his powers vanished. They were sucked away into Salamandra's staff. Eric could no longer do what he used to do.

He was normal and ordinary again.

He was . . . plain.

Eric hadn't told anyone yet. He couldn't bear to imagine how Julie and Neal would look at him. He felt bad enough already. But judging by his friends' excitement as he trotted up the library steps, he knew they'd soon be going back to Droon.

And then everyone would know.

"Let me guess," he said to them, "you both had dreams about Droon last night."

"We totally did," said Neal, laughing. "And that means we're going back. Today."

"What did you dream about?" Julie asked.

Eric frowned. "Tell me yours first?"

"Mine was weird," said Neal. "First I was looking at a beautiful blue sky. Then all of a sudden, this stream of smoke rises up. It's like a nutty dark finger or something. The way it wiggled, it looked like it was pointing at me and calling me over!"

"A finger of smoke pointed at you? Because you're a genie?" Eric asked.

"I think so," said Neal. "Anyway, it was very Droonian. Unless, of course, I was dreaming about the hot dog I grilled for breakfast yesterday. That smoked a lot, too."

Julie pulled open the library doors. The main room was already filled with people waiting for the rare books room to open.

"Our library is so cool," said Neal. "Plus, it's where all the books are!"

"Okay, now my turn," said Julie, passing through the crowd. "You know how they always say, 'Where there's smoke, there's fire'? Well, that's what I saw. Fire, moving like a giant finger over the land. It was a scary procession of torches."

Fingers. Fingers! thought Eric. *What's with all the fingers? I used to be able to shoot blasts of light from my fingers. But not anymore!*

"Interesting," he said. "I dreamed about a finger, too. It was pretty much the same."

"Was it smoke or fire?" asked Julie.

"Uh . . . water," said Eric.

He didn't want his friends asking him why he no longer had powers. He couldn't think of a way to tell them that didn't sound as if it were all his fault.

"Children, this way," called Mrs. Kroger

from across the room. "One last look around before we open the doors. Take a peek."

It was quiet and cool inside the rare books room. On the floor stood several glass-topped display cases draped in cloths to shield the expensive books from the light.

"The prize of our collection is this book here," Mrs. Kroger said. She lifted the cloth from one case where a leather book lay open, revealing two yellowed pages dense with inky handwriting and tiny drawings.

"It was donated to the library anonymously," she said. "We believe it's over five hundred years old. But there are others."

While Mrs. Kroger went over to one of the other cases, the children read the gold letters at the top of the page.

"*Sombraspina*," Julie whispered. "Eric, what does it mean? You know languages."

Not anymore! he thought. "Hmm. Let me think about that. . . ."

"Well, I've taken a little bit of Spanish," Julie said, "and I think *spina* might mean 'spine' or 'back.' *Sombra* probably means 'sleep.'"

"Maybe it means 'Go *Back* to *Sleep*,'" said Neal, "which is what my brain says whenever my alarm clock goes off."

"Don't I know it!" Mrs. Kroger chuckled.

All of a sudden, a yell came from outside the room. "Hey, everyone, look at that!"

"What's going on?" asked Julie.

When they ran back into the main room, they saw the crowd rushing outside. A woman was pointing across the lawn.

There, in the center of a perfectly blue sky, rose a narrow wisp of black smoke.

It looked exactly like a finger pointing.

"Holy crow!" gasped Neal. "My dream! I hope it doesn't call me over!"

Eric stood on his toes and saw the smoke rising behind the apple trees in his yard. "Guys, I think it's calling us all over. It's coming from my house. . . ."

A siren shrieked nearby, and the children raced away from the library. They cut through backyards until they saw two fire trucks screeching to a halt in front of Eric's house.

"Everyone, stay back!" yelled a firefighter, jumping down from one of the trucks. He motioned the gathering crowd away.

"Smoke filled the kitchen!" said Mrs. Hinkle, who was out on the front lawn. "It just came out of nowhere!"

"Oh, no! No . . . no . . ." said Eric. He ran to his mother. "Mom, I'm glad you're all right."

"I didn't see fire," she said. "Just smoke."

A trio of firefighters pulled a long hose across the lawn toward the kitchen door, while two others attached the far end to the nearest fire hydrant.

"Follow me," whispered Julie, pulling Eric by the arm. "We have to check out your basement."

Edging away from Mrs. Hinkle, the three friends scurried into the neighboring yard and peered through the hedge at Eric's small basement window.

"I can't see anything," said Neal.

"Let's get closer," said Julie.

Eric said nothing. He slipped under the hedge on his stomach, crawled to the basement window, and peered in. Smoke was streaming under the door of the closet under the stairs. It slithered like a snake across the basement floor and up to the kitchen.

"It's coming from Droon!" said Neal.

They heard men yelling and doors slamming on the far side of the house.

"The firefighters are in the kitchen," said Julie. "The second they see where the smoke is coming from, they'll find the closet. And the rainbow stairs. We need to get there first!"

"Okay," said Eric. Hands trembling, he pried up the basement window, slid onto his father's workbench, then jumped to the floor. Julie and Neal followed him. The room itself was not smoky.

"This isn't normal," said Julie, stepping over the stream of smoke and opening the closet door. "It's magic. It means something."

They switched on the light and entered the closet, careful not to step into the smoke moving across the floor. They closed the door behind them and turned off the light.

At once — *whoosh!* — the floor beneath them vanished and a long staircase appeared in its place. The usually bright steps were dulled by the smoke pouring up them.

"This is bad, people," said Neal. "Let's get down through the clouds as fast as we can."

But no sooner had they descended through the pink clouds than they froze in terror.

Ashes whirled everywhere. Through a storm of smoke, they saw Droon's pink-walled capital, Jaffa City — its towers, its fountains, the fabulous palace itself — completely swallowed by flames.

"No, no, no!" cried Eric.

A dark force of thousands of beasts, each bearing a blazing torch, circled about the city, laying siege to the walls.

"The torches in my dream!" gasped Julie.

Amid the torches were two tall spouts of green flame. They were twin fires from the horns of the bull-headed Emperor Ko!

All at once, they heard the distant cries of many people. Running toward the children, waving his wooden staff in excitement, was the wizard Galen, his blue cloak flying.

Behind him, Queen Relna, King Zello, Princess Keeah, and Max the spider troll were leading the entire population of Jaffa City up the stairs to safety.

"The worst has happened!" Max shouted to the children. "Fire! Destruction! From sea to sea — our beloved Droon is ablaze!"

Suddenly, the magnificent royal capital of Droon exploded in flames, then quaked and crashed to the ground.

Two

Take Two!

No sooner had the children watched the royal city crumble than — *whoosh!* — a fierce wind blew across the staircase. It pushed Eric into Julie and nearly toppled Neal off the steps altogether.

"Hold on!" yelled Julie. "Grab the rail!"

Bracing himself, Eric squinted down to see the black smoke scattering to ribbons.

"Hey, wait!" he gasped. "Look —"

The smoke billowed over the three

friends like an ocean wave, then dissolved to nothing.

The city they saw below them now was as pink and blue as ever. Its great wall stood firm and stout, the main square bustled with life, and the dome of the royal palace glittered in the sun. As always, the meadows outside the city were waving with bright, tall grass.

Most important, Galen, Zello, Relna, Keeah, Max, and the frightened crowd stampeding up the stairs were nowhere in sight. No trace of the terror they had just witnessed was visible.

"Uh . . . wait," said Julie. "We all saw that fire, didn't we? Because I saw it. I felt it!"

Neal sniffed his turban. "Except that my turban smells like my room at home. There's no smell of smoke. What just happened? Did we *imagine* that fire?"

The sound of flutes and harps broke

upon their ears. The king and queen entered the palace square to loud cheering. They bowed and began to dance.

"They're having a party?" said Julie.

"And didn't invite us?" said Neal. "Let's get down there. They probably have food!"

Neal and Julie quickly descended the steps to the bottom. Eric didn't.

"This isn't right," he said to himself. "None of this is right. My house . . ." He looked back to the top of the stairs and wondered if everything was all right at home.

He turned back to his friends, about to follow them down the stairs, when he saw a small object on the step at his feet.

He picked it up. He breathed deeply.

It was narrow, three inches long, polished brown, and had a needle-sharp point.

It was a thorn.

"Salamandra!" said Eric, his heart thudding in his chest. "It was *you*!"

He caught up with his friends in the main square just as Keeah ran to greet them all.

"You're right on time," she cried. "We're celebrating our return from Jabar-Loo!"

"And we've just begun!" boomed King Zello, twirling Queen Relna in his arms.

Keeah tried to draw Eric into the dancing crowd, but he broke away.

"Stop!" he yelled. "Everyone, stop!"

The princess raised her hand, and the music ceased. "What's wrong?" she asked.

"We just saw . . ." Eric tried to find the right words. "It was . . ."

"Jaffa City was on fire," said Julie. "We saw Ko's horns shooting green flames. It was horrible. He was burning the city to the ground. You were fleeing up the stairs to our world."

Queen Relna looked from one child to the other. "Did you all see this?"

Neal nodded. "We did. But then the vision vanished. None of it was real."

"Except for this . . ." said Eric. He opened his palm. "I found this thorn on the stairs. It means Salamandra the thorn princess was here. She likes visions. She made us see this terrible one."

Zello drew a large, knotted club from his waist. "Vision or no, if there is any chance Ko will attack Jaffa City, we'll give him a welcome he shall long remember! Guards, come! Jaffa City shall not burn!"

The king stormed off with a troop of soldiers. The blare of trumpets replaced the music of flutes and harps, and an alarm echoed throughout the city.

"If you had a vision of the future, we may yet have time to change it," said Keeah. "We have to tell Galen. He's in his tower."

Keeah quickly led Eric, Neal, and Julie to the wizard's tall tower inside a petrified tree.

The large, round chamber at the tower's summit was filled with books, maps, crystal balls, racks of weapons and wands, and shelves of wizard hats in several styles. To one side was a hazy-faced mirror on an ornate stand. It was the magical mirror that showed what was happening all over Droon.

Galen stood in the center of everything, leaning over a map of Droon. When the children entered, he looked up and smiled.

"Friends, welcome —"

The expressions on their faces stopped him. "Something serious. Tell me at once."

As the children explained their dreams

and their vision of the fire, and Eric showed the thorn he had found, Galen's face darkened. "A fiery vision of the future, was it? From our old friend Salamandra. I must call Max home from his gizzleberry festival. We need him."

Galen waved his hands and — *zzt-zzzt!* — the magic mirror awoke with a sizzling sound. A moment later, the surface cleared, and there was Max, standing on a mountaintop that shimmered pink in the sunlight.

"My little friend," said Galen to the mirror. "We need you here at once —"

"Ha!" chirped Max. "Not as much as *I* need *you* here at once!"

"What's happening?" asked Keeah.

The spider troll smiled. "I was passing the lovely Pink Mountains of Saleef when I spotted a rare starfox crying in distress among the crags."

"And being Max . . ." said Julie.

Max laughed. "And being me, I scrambled up the rocks to help him, only to find a tunnel cut deep into the mountain and the ancient symbols of Goll carved everywhere! Friends, I have discovered nothing less than the lair of Emperor Ko! He has secretly moved out of the Dark Lands and into Droon."

Eric had known it was only a matter of time before the evil emperor returned. For a while, the black-hearted leader of the beasts and his lieutenant, the moon dragon Gethwing, had been quiet. But now that Ko was in the vision of the attack on Jaffa City, and Max had found the emperor's lair, it was clear that Ko was on the move.

"And the rare starfox?" asked Galen.

"Perfectly fine," said Max, scooping up the silver-furred creature. "I found this stuck in his paw!"

He held up a long thorn.

"It's her again!" Eric gasped. "Salamandra!"

Eerrrrr! The silvery starfox sent up a loud wail.

"Salamandra —" Neal said.

Eerrrrr! the fox wailed.

"Salamandra —" Neal repeated.

Eerrrrr! Eerrrrr!

Galen laughed. "So our little starfox knows the Princess of Shadowthorn, too! Coincidence? I think not. Max, I suspect Salamandra led you to Ko's lair for a reason. Do not enter until we arrive. And I have just the thing to make our trip a quick one!"

Galen waved one hand over the mirror, and Max's image faded. Then the wizard leaned down, grabbed hold of the carpet under everyone's feet, and gave a sharp tug.

Flooop! The carpet — a large piece of

woven fabric fringed in gold — flattened out in the air and moved slowly toward the open window.

"Yes! The Pasha express!" said Keeah.

Flying rugs made by the magic-weaver Pasha were among the most priceless of all the enchanted objects in Droon. The friends piled onto the carpet and held on tight.

"And . . . fly!" said Galen.

Whoooosh! The carpet lurched out the window, and the five friends soared over Droon's sun-drenched countryside.

Before long, the fabulous peaks of the Mountains of Saleef came into view. They glistened rosy and pink in the sunlight.

From high up in the air, the children could just make out Max's bright orange hair as he waved up at them. Keeah landed the carpet on a peak near him and the starfox.

"Since we spoke, I have found something

else," said Max, calling them over to a chasm.

"More passages and thorns?" asked Neal.

"Stairs," said the spider troll. "And stairs for Emperor Ko are always dangerous!"

Everyone knew exactly what Max meant.

More than five hundred years before, Ko had built something called the Dark Stair from Droon to Salamandra's city of Pesh in the Upper World. He used it to kidnap Zara, the Queen of Light, and Sparr, her son, and bring them to Droon. The kidnapping was one of the most terrible events in Droon's history, but it was also the one that started the whole enchanted adventure, for Galen first came to Droon to search for his mother and brother.

Everyone stared at the narrow black steps carved into the walls of the chasm.

"The Dark Stair is sealed by a charm," said Galen. "I wonder where these steps lead."

"One thing we know," said Max. "They lead not up but down."

As they all peered at the darkness of the stairs, there came a whimper, and the starfox stumbled down the first step, then the second.

Errrrr! he wailed. When he tried to climb back up, he only slipped farther down.

"Help him!" shouted Keeah. She reached for the starfox but tripped. "Eric —"

Eric grabbed at her hand but couldn't manage to hold on, and he lost his balance. Julie, Neal, and Max reached for Eric and slipped, too.

Galen leaned down. "Take my hand!"

Even as Eric grabbed hold of Galen's hand, a fierce wind rushed down from behind them, pushing Keeah, Neal, Julie, and Max farther down the steps toward the starfox. As they fell, a stone door began to slide over the chasm's opening.

"Galen, save them!" cried Eric.

"Leave them!" snarled a sudden voice.

Eric's heart thudded. When he and Galen turned, they saw her.

Her.

Wearing a green cloak shimmering with scales and jewels, and wielding a staff of tangled thorns sizzling with sparks, was none other than Salamandra herself.

"Leave them," she repeated.

Her green-skinned face beamed as if in a smile, but her catlike eyes pierced theirs coldly.

As Keeah, Julie, Max, and Neal tumbled away into darkness, and the chasm shut above them, she began to laugh.

Three

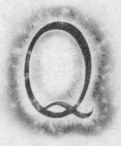

Her Again

"You again!" said Eric.

"Me again!" said the thorn-haired teenager.

"Princess of Shadowthorn!" said Galen.

"*Queen* of Shadowthorn, if you please," she said, spelling a big Q in the air with her finger. "I finally gave myself a promotion. Hey, I deserve it. I've been a princess for — what? — five thousand years? It's time I sat on a grown-up throne —"

"Enough!" said Galen abruptly. "Where are our friends?"

"Safe," she said. "Well, safe . . . ish. But you never know with Ko's hideouts. They have booby traps, mazes, surprises —"

"What are you up to now?" the wizard interrupted. "It was your little starfox that led Max to Ko's lair, wasn't it?"

"And you showed us a vision of Jaffa City on fire," said Eric. "Why?"

Salamandra pretended to faint. "Well, will you look at that! I try to be helpful, and this is the thanks I get. I feel so . . ."

"Evil?" said Galen.

"Misunderstood," she said with a laugh. "No, seriously, folks. I'm only trying to help."

In moments like these, listening to her joke around, Eric found it hard to believe that Salamandra really *was* evil. She had taken his powers, sure. And he desperately wanted them back. But she had helped him save his friends. In fact, she had helped to release Keeah's parents from the strange enchantments of Jabar-Loo. He just wasn't sure what she was up to — or why.

What really *was* going on in her mind?

"Salamandra, speak," said Galen.

The thorn queen strode to the edge of the crag and tapped the enormous block of stone that had sealed over their friends. Their distant cries could still be heard.

"I stumbled through a ragged hole in the fabric of time," she said. "Never mind how. But I saw a future full of fire and smoke. All was chaos, unclear, dark. And yet I *felt* something I believe was Ko. Good girl that I am, I thought you should know."

"Ko plans to attack Jaffa City?" said

Eric. "To burn it like in the vision you sent us?"

"For starters," she said. "But I think we can stop him."

Galen glared at her. "Why do you care?"

"That's for me to know and you to find out," she said. "In the meantime, I can tell you that if Ko is eliminated now, Droon can be saved. For the moment."

Eric and Galen stood staring at the thorn queen, stunned into silence. Finally, the wizard spoke. "And *how* is he to be eliminated?"

Salamandra's face twisted into a smile. "You remember my fabulous Portal of Ages, don't you? Using it, I can send Ko back into the distant past, trapping him in time. I can make him a prisoner forever. The problem is that the Portal lies hidden beyond sight. To locate it I need the silver thorn. Find the silver thorn for me, and the great war of fire and destruction I see coming will be delayed until Sparr returns. Sparr is needed in that war if Droon is to be saved."

Sparr? Eric felt as if an ice cube had slid down his back. Salamandra had once come to him in a vision asking about Sparr. He had told her that Sparr had vanished.

"Is that why you came to me?" asked Eric. "To find out about Sparr? Are you saying that Sparr will come back?"

Her eyes flashed. "If you help me and we act now, yes. Sparr returns."

"Help you?" said Galen. "We barely trust you! What if we do *not* help you now?"

She turned to him. "I've been in Ko's lair. I know where your friends are trapped —"

"So!" boomed Galen. "You are forcing us! You . . . you . . . *person!*"

The children's calls echoed beneath

the block of stone. Galen stormed off toward it.

Eric had turned to join him when Salamandra grabbed his arm. She narrowed her eyes. "Why, Eric Hinkle, you little secret-keeper!" she whispered. "What will your friends say when they discover you lost your magic —"

"Lost it? You saw to that!" he snapped. "When will I get my powers back? If we do this for you, will I be a wizard again?"

"That's up to you," she said. "Losing your powers was the price for saving Droon."

"But for how long? And what does that mean anyway?"

"It means . . . hush!"

Galen returned from the sealed chasm, dejected and angry. He stared at the queen. "So where is this silver thorn you need?"

Salamandra grinned. "Oh, goodie. I knew you'd agree to find it. It's in Pesh!"

Eric nearly choked. "Pesh? Your ancient traveling city in the Upper World? The silver thorn is in Pesh?!"

"A little outside, actually," she said. "From the eastern gate, you take a right, then hang a left through the foothills. Five hundred years ago, my goblins were bringing the thorn to me when Ko attacked them. That magic thorn disappeared on the very night Ko marched up the Dark Stair and entered the Upper World. Maybe you know about that night —"

Galen's face turned pale. "That night . . . that very night . . ." he murmured. He closed his eyes for a moment. When he opened them, they were brimming with tears. "On the very night Ko kidnapped my mother and my brother Sparr?"

Salamandra tilted her head. "Oh, right!

That happened, too. So, look. Bring me the thorn, and you'll have your revenge."

"But the Dark Stair to Pesh is sealed shut," said Eric. "We can't get there anymore."

"There's another way," she said. "Long ago, a secret book was written about my empire of Shadowthorn and its capital, Pesh. That book still exists, passed down through the ages, tumbled from one hand to another until now. Until this very day."

"Where do we find it?" asked Galen.

She shrugged, then said brightly, "Try looking where all the books are!"

Eric stared at Salamandra. *Where all the books are?* Neal had said that earlier.

"You mean the library?" he asked.

She smiled. "To reveal what is hidden, sometimes all you have to do is pull the veil aside."

"You speak in riddles!" said Galen. "What do you mean?"

"I mean time moves fast," she snapped. "Ko gains strength. Your friends need air! And you'll need them. They're part of Droon's future, just as Sparr is. Now, go!"

With a wave of her staff, Salamandra created a funnel of spinning thorns around herself. A moment later — *poooom!* — she was gone, and the mountaintop was littered with steaming thorns.

"Can we trust her?" said Eric. "Galen?"

"We have a mission," the wizard said abruptly. Standing over the sealed chasm, he struck the stone with his palm. "Friends! Be safe until we return. And we *shall* return!"

Then he unrolled the flying carpet, turned to Eric, and said, "Come!"

Leaping onto the carpet, the two friends flew up from the mountaintop and soared back over the plains toward Jaffa City.

Four

Up the Stairs

Eric and Galen soared as swiftly as the magic carpet would carry them to the place where the rainbow stairs had last appeared.

"Whose side is Salamandra on?" asked Eric.

"Her own," said Galen, leaning into the wind. "Make no mistake. Salamandra does nothing that does not help herself."

Eric looked back at the pink-stoned

peaks. He knew it was true. And yet she *had* helped them in the past. She was irritating and confusing, but could her side really be their side, too? Or was she just helping herself now?

Maybe. Or . . . maybe not. He wasn't sure.

The walls of Jaffa City sparkled in the sun, even as great numbers of soldiers patrolled its thick walls. Galen tugged the carpet, and it lifted into the sky, slowed, and then stopped in midair.

"I don't like to do this, but . . ." The wizard tossed a handful of glittering dust high into the air. It struck something invisible but solid, revealing a set of curving stairs.

"The staircase!" said Eric. "You found it!"

Galen nodded. "It has faded from sight, but is still here. Let us hurry up."

They leaped onto the stairs. On Galen's command, the carpet remained hovering. The two friends were at the top seconds before the steps faded from view once more.

Opening the closet door, they found Eric's basement empty. A warm patch of sunlight brightened the floor. As Eric guessed, there was no sign of smoke anywhere. "It's clear," he whispered, slipping out of the closet.

"You have an idea where we might find this strange book Salamandra has told us about?" Galen asked.

Eric smiled despite himself. "The library. Where all the books are," he said. "And I know where to look. We have a new rare books room. It has display cases with cloths over them."

"Ah, pull the veil aside to reveal what is hidden!" said Galen with a smile.

"Salamandra may send people on chases, but she does give clues. Perhaps first, though, a change of clothes?" The wizard motioned to his blue cloak. "And of size and face, too? We should arouse no suspicion at all."

In an instant, Galen shrank away, and the figure standing in his place was Neal!

"Holy crow!" Eric gasped. "Galen, I don't know. Neal's mom is the librarian, you know."

The wizard smiled. "The better to get into secret places. I shall be on my best behavior."

Eric laughed. "Funny, Neal never is." Carefully closing the closet door, he led the wizard up the basement stairs to his kitchen, then out the side door to his front lawn. "You'll need to use some of Neal's key words to convince his mom. He says *dude* and *whoa* and *totally* a lot. Also *burger, hot dog, peanut butter*, and anything to do with food. Plus he likes baseball and basketball. A lot."

"Those are foods, too?" Galen asked.

Eric looked at him. "Uh . . . no. Sports," he said. "Though he's not good at either of them. I'm better. And Julie's better than both of us. But don't try to tell him that."

Eric could go on and on, telling Galen more things about Neal, but time was running out. If what Salamandra had told them was actually true, they had to find the silver thorn in the few minutes before Ko did, or her plan to send the beast emperor to the past would fail.

Hurrying through the streets unnoticed, Eric and Galen soon arrived at the library. They rushed into the main reading room and through the waiting crowd outside the rare books room. Because almost no time had passed since Eric and his friends had left for Droon, the room hadn't yet opened to the public.

Only Mrs. Kroger was inside.

Eric nudged Galen as they opened the door. "Remember what I told you. And be cool."

"Boys," said Neal's mother, turning when they entered the room. "I think everything's ready —"

"Whoa, dude!" Galen said. "Dog me a hot peanut burger! I totally love basketbase!"

Mrs. Kroger's jaw dropped. "Excuse me?"

Eric pulled the wizard aside and whispered, "Not so weird! If you can't be Neal, just be you!"

Galen nodded. "Got it." With a big smile, he bowed and took Mrs. Kroger's hand. "Forgive the silliness, Mother. We have come to consult the ancient books. They are very educational, you know." He stepped over to the display cases.

Mrs. Kroger made a face at Eric. "Is Neal . . . sick . . . or something?"

Eric tried to laugh. "No, no. Earlier we found a book about manners. He's trying to be more polite."

She frowned, then smiled. "Well, that's probably a good thing. He should read more."

She looked at the clock, nodded, then left the room, closing the door behind her.

"I suppose I overdid it?" the wizard asked with a chuckle.

"A little bit," said Eric. "But being Neal is something only one person has ever been able to do. Over here —"

They went straight for the case at the

far end of the room. Eric lifted the cloth away, and the old book that he, Neal, and Julie had seen lay open as before.

Galen breathed deeply. "We must remove it for a moment." He ran his hand over the case. Its lock clicked, and the case popped open.

The wizard's hands shook as he touched the ancient pages.

"*Sombraspina*," he whispered.

"We thought it was about sleep," said Eric. "But maybe not?"

"Not quite," said Galen. "*Sombraspina* is a word made up of two Spanish words. *Sombra* and *espina* . . . shadow . . . thorn."

Eric trembled, and yet somehow he wasn't surprised. The book seemed far too mysterious simply to be about sleep. "It just showed up here at the library."

Galen turned to him. "For a reason, I have no doubt. Eric, when you return here later, you must find out how this book arrived here. Where it came from. Who owned it. You *must* find out."

Eric stared at the book. "I will."

The smell of ancient days wafted over them when Galen turned the pages. He stopped at a fanciful drawing. Right away they recognized it as the ancient city of Pesh.

Galen bent over the drawing. "So . . . not all magic is lost from your world as we thought," he said. "This book contains a power you may never have dreamed of."

"What do you see?" asked Eric.

"Look for yourself!"

When Eric studied the drawing closely, he saw streets drawn in delicate detail, weaving away into the distance. Canals, bridges, the great dark palace — it all seemed more like a fantastic photograph than a sketch.

All of a sudden, he jumped. "That person . . . he moved! I saw him move!"

Galen nodded excitedly. "Yes! Yes! *Sombraspina* turns out to be quite a magic book, after all. Look near the palace wall. . . ."

As Eric moved his eyes slowly across the drawing, he saw a wagon roll down a tiny street. Overhead, a tiny bird swooped, then dipped into a square. A banner, black and purple as the night, waved, and then . . .

And then he saw two figures by the palace wall. The tall one wore a cloak and coned hat. The smaller figure of a boy stood next to him.

"Wait," he said. "Is that . . . us? It's us!"

As he watched, the two figures moved, first one way, then the other, as if they were searching for something.

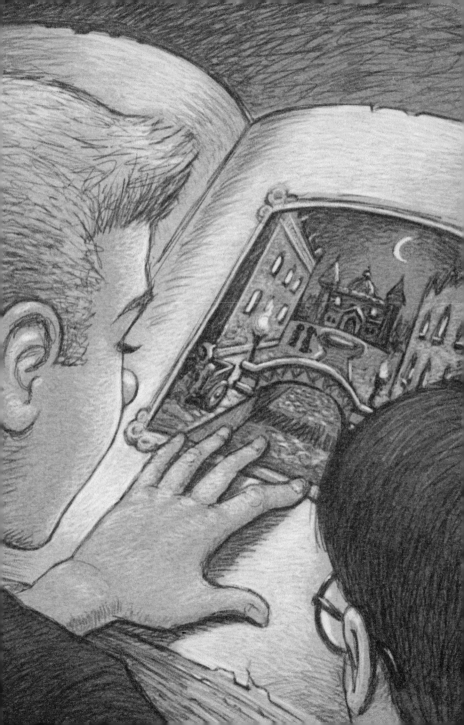

All of a sudden, the drawing seemed to move toward him, filling his vision.

"Galen —!" he said. He reached wildly for the wizard's hand, but Galen was right there with him, holding his hand tightly.

Whether the two friends were falling toward the page, or the picture was growing up around them, he couldn't tell, but the room, the library, the town, his world — all were falling backward away from him.

At the same time, the city of Pesh was growing huge in front of him.

The wizard's iron grip held him until the pull from the drawing was too strong and together they fell, fell, fell.

The next instant, Eric and Galen were standing together on a winding cobbled street in the foul-smelling shadows of the great palace of Pesh!

Five

A Mesh in Pesh

"That was . . . my gosh! I don't even know!" gasped Eric. "What is that book?"

With a wave of his hand, Galen's face aged, his beard grew out, and as quick as a wink he was Neal no longer. "A relic of a former time. A secret of untold power. And one you must keep safe at all costs."

The wizard scanned the dark street, moved into the shadows, and pulled Eric with him, his eyes darting in every direction. "Whether Salamandra has become good, remains bad, or is somewhere in between is a judgment we cannot make just yet. But one thing is for sure. Her street-leaping, net-flinging, and carpet-flying goblins are all around us. It would be bad luck indeed if we ran afoul of them. If the plains outside are where the silver thorn was lost, we must exit the city as quickly and quietly as possible. This way."

The farther they moved through the narrow streets, the more Eric's fear of Salamandra's dark city returned, and the more he reflected upon how his world and Droon were first linked together.

The story began in the Upper World. And in many ways it began with Salamandra.

Her flight through the Portal of Ages

had landed her city of Pesh in the very place and time that Galen and Eric found themselves at that moment. She had come for one reason alone: to steal magic.

Learning of Salamandra's evil intentions, the wizard Zara, Queen of Light, along with her young sons, Urik and Galen, and their infant brother, Sparr, had come to stop her.

Unknown to them, Ko, the beast emperor of Goll, was drawn to the Upper World by tales of Zara's astonishing magic. He built the terrible Dark Stair from Droon to this world. That very night, Ko would find Zara's camp outside Pesh. He would kidnap her and her infant son and take them back to Droon.

Now Eric and Galen were in Pesh just before all that happened.

Before all that happened.

Eric realized something he had not before. "Ko hasn't yet attacked your mother's camp yet. It hasn't happened yet, so . . ."

The wizard frowned. "Yes, at this very moment, my mother is safe in her camp among the hills. My infant brother, Sparr, still sleeps in her arms. Urik and I slumber nearby, ignorant of any danger."

Eric trembled at the thought that he had next. "So . . . you can stop Ko. . . ."

Galen breathed in sharply. "If I witnessed his terrible deed, I would have no power to stop myself."

"You *shouldn't* stop yourself. It was evil —"

Like a sudden storm, Galen grew angry, though Eric could tell he was not angry with him. "No! That terrible kidnapping was the one event that brought our worlds together! If I reversed it, if I thwarted Ko now, none of our history — as painful as much of it has been — would have happened. Remember this, Eric. What befell us that night — Ko's coming into this world, his stealing of Zara and Sparr and bringing them to Droon — was all a surprise."

"It was terrible," said Eric.

"But listen here!" Galen went on. "Would Droon ever have been known if I hadn't devised the rainbow staircase to search for my mother and Sparr? Would it?"

Eric was dumbfounded. "I . . . I . . ."

"You struggle with the answer," the wizard said gently. "I have struggled with it every day of my life. Remember that we are in the past. The tiniest change here could affect the future in startling ways. The single flap of a butterfly's wings can grow and grow until it becomes a storm. Remember that. Let us do what we came for and no more. No more."

Eric nodded. He was glad Galen was

with him. He knew that when the time came he could tell the wizard about the loss of his powers. He *would* tell him.

Not yet, he thought. *But soon, very soon* . . .

All at once, there came a sound of footsteps slapping across the rooftops above them, and a glimmer of green light moved across the cobblestones ahead.

"Goblins!" hissed Galen. He crouched, his fingers flashing with sparks.

Eric stumbled in the shadows, and the green light flooded over him.

"There! There! Spies!" cried a goblin.

All at once — *whooomf!* — a heavy black net fell toward them from the rooftop above.

"Eric, run! Find the thorn!" Galen cried.

"What? No, both of us —"

"It's too late!" said Galen. He pushed

Eric to safety, then fell under the net himself. It slithered over him as if it were alive, trapping his hands so he couldn't blast his way free.

As goblins leaped down from the roofs, Eric pulled Galen to his feet and hustled him into a side alley. "I . . . I can't free you from the net!" he said, nearly in tears. "I lost all my magic. I made this mess. I should have told you —"

"I knew," said Galen, stumbling forward.

"What?"

"The moment you entered Droon, I knew."

"Then why did you save me on the mountaintop?" Eric asked. "Why not Neal or Julie or Keeah? They all have powers! They could have helped!"

Galen groaned as the net tightened on

him, and the goblins hurried closer. He fixed his eyes on Eric and smiled. "Why do you think?"

"But I . . . I . . . have no magic anymore!"

"Nothing great is ever easy," said the wizard. "But of all the magics I possess, being human is the most powerful. And that is what is needed here. Ignore my mother's tent. Find the thorn. Do your best. Remember everything we have said. And go!"

The wizard spun around haltingly and drew the goblins away. Eric stared after him for a moment, then turned and ran as fast as he could down the side alley.

Just before he climbed to the nearest roof, he saw the goblin horde trap Galen, hoist him up, and carry him roughly toward the palace.

Six

Through Billowing Curtains

When Eric reached the city wall, he turned. "Thank you, Galen," he whispered. "I'll be back for you."

Then he climbed over the parapet and jumped ten feet to the damp ground outside. Breathing hard, he set his sights on the plains stretching out darkly beyond.

Pull the veil aside, he thought. *Reveal what is hidden. Ignore the tent. Wings of a butterfly!*

He was pretty sure he didn't understand any of it.

"Well," he said to himself, "if nothing great is ever easy, and this sure won't be easy, maybe it'll turn out to be great!" He nearly laughed at his own words, but the wail of goblins from inside the city startled him back to himself. He decided to put those thoughts away and do what had to be done.

"*Try* to do what has to be done," he said to himself. "Find the silver thorn."

Eric moved quickly away from the city. A path, not well defined but passable, zig-zagged into the foothills. He ran up it until he reached the peak of the lowest hill. From its far side he saw black plains rolling away as far as the horizon.

Searching the ground below, he spotted a small campfire smoldering under a broad shelf of rock, its embers blinking like cats' eyes in the dark.

"Have I found Ko already?" he wondered. "Or more goblins?" Then he saw three horses with golden saddles, and his heart fluttered.

He crept carefully down the hill until he could see directly under the ledge. A large blue tent sat nestled at the foot of the hill. Its billowing silken walls and upthrust posts were nearly hidden among the rocks.

Eric stared at it for minutes in silence, then whispered softly to the night. "Queen Zara is in there! And young Galen and Urik, and even Sparr, no more than an infant!"

As always when Eric spoke the name of Galen's mother, he felt an ache in his chest. He had often thought of it as something like being pierced by an arrow, but that wasn't right, for it both hurt and did not hurt.

Then he remembered Salamandra's words about pulling aside the veil, and they seemed not so much about the cloth over the library's display case as about the silken tent flap.

He felt drawn to the little camp with every part of his being. He knew he was only a few hundred feet away from seeing something he had never imagined he would see: all of the wizards together.

Galen had told him to ignore the tent, but he could just as soon stop breathing!

He darted from rock to rock until he was on the ground not twenty paces from the tent. The horses raised their heads to gaze at him, then lowered them again, making no noise.

Eric moved lightly over the ground until he stood at the tent's flap. He reached out his hand and pulled the cloth gently aside.

He nearly cried out.

Queen Zara was asleep, the baby Sparr

at her side. Young Galen slumbered nearby, wrapped in silken blankets. But Urik, the eldest of the three brothers, sat at a makeshift desk, a tiny lit candle by his elbow.

He was writing with a feathered quill, pausing, writing some more. And the book he was writing in . . . was . . . was . . . the big brown book at Eric's own library!

Eric's knees gave out, and he sank to the ground. He stared at the book. Was it the same book? It was the same! How could it be? How could Urik's book be at his own library?

Urik's book! How did it get there? How!

He rose to his feet and leaned forward to speak, to tell Urik what was coming, when a faint sound came from the hill above him.

Looking up, Eric saw a spurt of green fire.

He released the tent cloth. It fluttered closed.

"Ko's horns!" Eric said to himself. "He's here. The horrible beast is here!"

Stepping silently away from the tent, Eric scrambled back up the hill and saw Ko storming this way and that in the pass above, waving his four arms in every direction over the countryside. A trio of red-faced Ninn warriors stood nearby, watching their leader nervously.

Eric knew that the Ninns were part of the story, too. Legends told of how Ko had forced the peaceful, blue-skinned Orkins to build the Dark Stair. Under Ko's influence, the Orkins turned evil and became Ninns.

Ko shuddered from horns to hooves, then began to speak. "O Queen of Light!" he said. "O Wizard Mother of the Upper World, I have heard of you. I have come for you. My charms shall bind your great magic to mine!"

"Where is she, O master?" one Ninn asked.

"Near!" said Ko. "We shall find her!"

Eric's heart ached when he thought about the sad history to come. Ko *had* found Zara. He *had* charmed her, and the charm had ended her life.

Eric could feel anger rising up in him. All the history of Droon would be changed if he could stop Ko right here, right now.

Could he do it? Should he do it?

"Emperor, look there!" said one of the Ninns. "A caravan in the night! With magic!"

Ko swung his giant head to the east. A narrow line of torches slithered in the distance, coming toward the foothills.

Eric stood as tall as he could on the hilltop. Squinting, he saw a group of twenty or so goblins tramping in a line. The middle ones carried a small jeweled chest.

"Goblins bring more magic to Salamandra of Pesh!" said the second Ninn.

"It shall be mine!" said Ko. His horns spouted flames again, and Eric guessed that the beast's greed for magic had gotten the better of him. "First the treasure, then the queen!"

It all happened in the blink of an eye. Ko and his Ninns rushed to the pass's far end and swooped upon the unsuspecting caravan. Salamandra's forces were no match for the emperor's magical fury. He sent a storm upon them. Many goblins ran away in fear. Those that didn't were charmed by Ko into a tangle of their own tails. While the Ninn warriors chased the goblins into the plains, Emperor Ko knelt down by the small chest.

Eric crept to the end of the pass and saw

that the chest was covered by a silver cloth.

Pull the veil aside! Again!

Ko's mighty claws were about to do just that when Eric stood up and called out. "No you don't, Ko! That chest belongs to Salamandra, and I need it!"

Though he felt no electricity in his fingers as he normally did, his heart was pumping wildly as he ran toward Ko. He leaped off the hill right down at the horned emperor. The force of his leap knocked Ko to the ground, but the beast was up in a flash.

"Who dares attack the great Ko, Master of Droon?" the beast boomed. Not waiting for an answer, he sent a blazing fireball through the air. Eric dived to the dirt, and the blast struck the ground behind him. Ko charmed a second fireball, larger than the first, but Eric hurled himself at the little chest, ripped its cloth aside, and was nearly blinded by the silver light. He plunged his hand into the light and grasped the thorn that lay inside the chest.

It sliced his fingers, but he held it tight.

"You shall not steal from Ko!" shouted the emperor, rushing forward.

Eric turned on his heel and ran blindly in the night, then nearly choked when he realized he was running straight for Zara's tent.

He stopped short and turned.

"No!" he cried out. "You can't! You can't!"

But it was too late. Ko had seen Zara's tent.

With a flick of his massive fist, Ko thrust the boy aside like a rag doll. Eric hit his head on a rock and was out for a moment. When he came to, Ko and his Ninns were

ripping fiercely at the tent. It happened in flashes of green fire and yelling. There was a baby's scream, a groan of pain, then it was over.

"Back to Droon with the queen and her son!" cried Ko, cradling the limp forms of Zara and Sparr in two arms, while pounding his chest in a howl of terrifying joy with the others. Moments later he and his Ninns descended the Dark Stair and were gone.

"No!" Eric cried, staring at the tent, its posts broken, its silks tattered. He knew that Urik and Galen were frozen in a trance inside the tent. When they came out of it, they would search Pesh for their mother, not knowing she had been spirited away to Droon.

Eric fell to his knees and slammed the ground with his fists. "No! No! *Why?*"

But it had already happened. It was over.

His heart heavy, full of anger, he knew he could do nothing but continue his mission. He turned away from the foothills and ran all the way back to Pesh. He knew the weight of silver in his hand was magical. He could feel it pulsing in his palm. He knew it was Salamandra's magic and not his own that allowed him to enter Pesh unseen and walk the streets as if he were invisible. Twice he thought goblins had spotted him, only to walk on unhindered.

Unseen, he entered the dark palace; unseen, he found Galen's dungeon. He unlocked the heavy door and led the wizard through the narrow passages. When Galen emerged from the palace, Eric was already running ahead into the shadowy streets.

"You have done well," Galen said when they finally reached the spot where they had entered Pesh.

Eric breathed deeply, then hung his head. "Let's just get out of here."

The wizard held him by the shoulder. "Eric, your face tells me you could do nothing."

"Wrong," said Eric angrily. "I did do something! I led Ko right to your tent! I did it! I did it! It's all my fault —"

Galen turned away for a moment. "You . . ." Then he shook his head. "No. It happened as it had to happen. If you had had your powers, you might have tried to stop Ko. You might have alerted my brother, my mother, me. You and I would now be strangers. You would not have become the wizard you are!"

Eric's heart thumped in anger. "Well, I'm not a wizard! I'm nothing now —"

"As if flashy powers make a wizard!" said Galen, with a hint of a smile on his lips. "But you will see that more clearly in time. Here is the corner where we saw our-selves in the drawing. Move this way . . . that way . . . yes . . ."

The moment the two of them moved as they had in the drawing, the picture dissolved around them, and they were back in the library, Galen looking like Neal once more.

Seeing the book safely back in its case, Eric told Galen what he had seen in the tent.

"Urik's book?" said the wizard. "But how did it come to be here? Eric, we must know —"

But they could not linger. Mrs. Kroger entered, and the crowd came in behind her.

With great effort, Eric smiled at her, though his smile disappeared as soon as she turned away.

"That crusty book is totally whoa," Galen said to her. "I can really learn a lot!"

Mrs. Kroger seemed surprised. "Maybe it will help you get an A in Spanish."

"Maybe I'll get three As!" said Galen.

Eric pulled him away. "Which means we'd better go study now! Bye, Mrs. K!"

They rushed quickly out of the library, the smile on Mrs. Kroger's face lasting longer than Eric had ever seen.

Seven

There and Back Again

Eric raced home, with Galen following hard on his heels. They saw no one, didn't stop to catch their breath, and were soon in his basement closet. When the stairs appeared, they descended. All this was done without saying a word.

Eric could think of nothing to say.

So this was his life without powers? Messing up? Doing things that only went wrong?

If this was being plain old Eric, he hated it.

He rushed headlong down the rainbow stairs. Obedient to Galen's command, the flying carpet still hovered in the air next to the stairs. Eric plopped down on it, followed by the wizard. A short, silent ride later, they arrived at the foot of the Pink Mountains of Saleef.

"Eric, wait —" Galen started, when they hopped off the carpet together. But he couldn't get the rest out, for suddenly — *ba-boooom!* — the pink stone erupted violently.

Galen just managed to wrap the carpet around Eric protectively when a wave of dust rolled over them. Before the dust cleared, someone spoke.

"Master!"

Max stepped out of the dust, coughing.

He ran straight to Galen. "It was ... it was ..."

"Awesome!" said Keeah, running out next.

Neal and Julie stumbled out with her, followed by Salamandra and the little starfox.

"It was amazing!" said Neal. "I drove Ko's beasts nuts by floating over their heads every time they tried to grab me."

"I was nearly caught," said Julie, "but Salamandra saved me with her staff. Then I changed into a snake and scared the beasts."

"We escaped them!" said Max. "Yay!"

"Not quite," said Galen. "Look there."

Deep in the mountain's hole a crowd of beasts, their eyes glimmering in the darkness, were rushing out toward the friends.

Even as Galen raised his sparking fingertips, Salamandra whirled on her heels.

"I've got it!" she said, shaking her staff.

Blam! — a hedge of thorns grew instantly over the hole, sealing the beasts inside.

"They'll soon find another way out," the queen said. She turned toward Eric and her eyes fell on the silver thorn. "Ooh, my magic! Now stand aside, everyone, and see what I can do!" She snatched the thorn from Eric and strode away. Placing the silver thorn on the ground, she began to murmur words under her breath.

"You're welcome," Eric grumbled.

Galen turned to Julie. "And what have you found there?" he asked.

Julie shrugged. "I'm not exactly sure," she answered. Cradled in her hands was a heavy black stone the size and shape of a softball. It was veined with blue and red threads of light, and it seemed to shimmer from inside.

"We found this all by itself in a secret chamber," she said. "Something about it attracted me. Maybe it can tell us where Ko is planning his terrible attack."

Galen held the stone to his ear, shook it, then sniffed it. "It is curiously heavy. A magic ball of some sort. If it was in Ko's chamber, it may indeed give us a clue as to where he is."

"So what happened in Pesh?" asked Neal.

Eric wanted to forget what happened in Pesh, but as soon as he opened his mouth, he couldn't stop. "I totally messed up, that's what happened!" he said. "I got Galen captured. I led Ko right to Zara's tent. She was kidnapped because of me. I have no powers. No magic. Salamandra took it all!"

He pointed at the thorn queen.

She looked up at him, her eyes flashing, then bent over her silver thorn again.

Eric felt like crying, but he held it in.

"Anyway . . ." he said. "Now you know. That's the secret I've been keeping from you."

"Eric, it's terrible to lose your magic," said Keeah, putting her hand on his arm. "But I'm sure you'll get it back. More importantly, you found the thorn."

"We needed it," said Julie. "You did good."

"Totally," said Neal. "Thanks to you, we'll stop Ko."

Galen spoke. "Eric found the silver thorn. A nearly impossible task, but that was our mission, and that's what Eric did. And he did it all on his own."

"Well, good job," said Neal, folding his turban into his pocket.

"Ah, that reminds me," said Galen. "Neal, speaking of a good job, I think you'll have to do a good job in school for a while."

Neal turned pale. "What happened?"

"Galen had to think of a disguise," said Eric, almost smiling despite himself. "And he chose to be you. He talked to your mother."

"Uh-oh," said Neal nervously. "Did Mom believe it was me?"

Galen nodded. "Certainly. But . . . she is expecting A work from you."

"No way," said Neal. "You told her not to expect an A, right?"

"I told her to expect three!" said Galen.

Neal groaned. "Talk about doing the impossible!"

The thorn queen turned to face them. "Enough jibber-jabber! Get ready to take a trip, folks! The silver thorn may be old, but watch what it can do!"

With a loud explosion and a puff of green smoke, the tiny silver thorn began to grow and grow. Soon it was as large as a boat. Its top flattened into a deck, and with a wrenching sound, a mast sprouted from its center. A sail fluttered down from its top. The hull was lifted from the ground by six giant, wooden-spoked wheels, three on each side.

A big flat rudder jutted off the back, and a figurehead emerged from the front. It was a carving of Salamandra's own head. Its eyes were bright emeralds that shone in the dark. Its mane was a thorny, tangle of eel-like tresses. The small silver thorn had become an enormous, wheeled boat.

"Behold the Landboat of Pesh!" Salamandra said. "It's our way to the Portal of Ages!"

"Not bad," said Galen softly.

"Coming from you, that's a compliment,"

Salamandra said with a toothy grin. She stood beside the Landboat and began to stroke its silver hull. "According to an ancient legend, the Landboat will take us to the place where the Portal of Ages lies hidden. Landboat, do your stuff!"

The giant masted thorn stirred suddenly. Its sail billowed, and it moved slowly across the stony ground, first one way, then the other.

At the same time, Julie gasped. "Oh!"

The black orb jumped in her hands, pulling one way, then the other.

"What's happening?" asked Keeah.

Julie closed her eyes as if in a trance. "This orb," she said. "It's telling me something. . . . I think it knows where Ko is. . . ."

At the same instant, the Landboat jerked to a stop, and Julie froze where she stood.

"The boat points south toward . . ."

Salamandra blurted. Her voice sounded strange, as if she were possessed.

"This orb is pointing toward . . ." said Julie.

"The Dust . . ." Salamandra continued.

". . . Hills . . ." Julie breathed.

". . . of Panjibarrh!" they said together.

Before anyone had time to think — *krrrrkkk!* — the Landboat began to roll across the ground away from the pink mountains.

"It's going to the Dust Hills!" cried Max. "Everyone in the Landboat. All aboard!"

Eight

Journey of the Landboat

At a word from Salamandra, wind blew up from nowhere and filled the sail. The Landboat took off, bouncing and bumping over the plains like a giant wagon.

"Ahhhh!" cried Neal, clinging to the mast. "And I mean — *ahhhhh!*"

"At this speed, we'll be seeing the Hills soon!" said Max, his eyes fixed on the horizon. "I hope King Batamogi and his people are safe."

Batamogi and his nine brothers were kings of the Oobja mole people, a tribe of furry hill dwellers with old customs and peaceful ways.

Salamandra laughed as the wind whipped her tangled mop of hair every which way. She aimed her magic staff behind the craft. Thorns shot from it like rocket thrusters, propelling the Landboat ever faster across the plains.

Eric had thought that after he told everyone about the loss of his powers, he would feel better.

Instead, he felt worse.

Keeah, Julie, and Neal were crowded together on the bow, gazing into the distance. Eric knew it was wrong, but he couldn't help imagining that they were growing closer to one another and leaving him out.

He edged nearer to them and listened.

"Something's happening in the hills," Julie was telling the others. "I can sense it. I hear scratching and clawing. Someone is talking. A lot of people are talking, chattering. And running. There are echoes. I think the Oobja people are . . . hiding . . . underground."

"Hiding? How do you know?" asked Keeah.

"This is going to sound like Neal," said Julie. "I don't know *how* I know, but I know I *know*. You know what I mean?"

I do! Eric reflected bitterly.

"Cool," said Neal, grinning. "Maybe when Salamandra helped you with her staff, some of her magic rubbed off on you."

Or some of my *magic!* thought Eric.

Keeah nodded. "I'm sure it will help us."

Because I can't? Eric thought.

All of a sudden, there came a terrible cracking noise, and darkness dropped on them as heavily as a stone.

"What's happening?" cried Max, waving at the black air. "Galen —"

The wizard thrust his staff into the air, but its brilliant colors were not enough to penetrate the darkness. "This is some sort of magic shroud. Salamandra?"

The thorn queen shot a fireball from her thorn staff, but it, too, vanished. At the same time, they heard the sound of heavy wings thundering overhead in the darkness.

"Gethwing?" shouted Keeah. "Is it the moon dragon? Is it? Is he helping Ko?"

But they couldn't see. As fog shrouded the ship, stinging their eyes, claws flashed out of the darkness and struck the mast as if trying to pluck it out.

"Beast, show yourself!" cried Galen.

Eric took cover near Keeah as she braced

herself against the hull and fired sparks into the air.

Blam! Blam!

Salamandra thrust her magic staff here and there, and fiery thorns shot into the sky. Galen kept whacking at the air with his staff.

There was a yowl of pain, a loud flapping of wings, then nothing.

The Landboat rolled to a stop, and the fog cleared. No one was hurt, but shards of the black orb were scattered across the deck.

"Whatever it was tried to steal the orb," said Max. "When it couldn't, it destroyed it!"

Galen stooped to the deck and collected the ball's fragments. "Which means this object was important enough to destroy. Perhaps time will tell us what it means."

"Time tells me one thing already!" said Salamandra, looking to the skies. "It's passing. We must launch the Landboat once more!"

Thrust by another magical wind, the boat took off again. It arrived in Panjibarrh just as night fell and the moon rose on the horizon.

As Julie had predicted, the Oobja village was deserted. The dust-covered hills rolled away in every direction, but they were barren of the mole people who normally lived there.

Salamandra stopped the Landboat, scooped up the starfox, and led the small crew into the empty village. "Ko's dark plans are hatching even now. My Portal of Ages is close. Already I see a hapless soul drawn into it, a prisoner of the past unable to escape!"

Eric glanced at Galen, who shared his look.

"Perhaps we should send Ko back all the way to the Shadow Time," Max suggested. "It's when he was born, after all."

"Perhaps," said Salamandra. "The Portal of Ages goes anywhere and any time."

Turning, she chanted over the Landboat, and it shrank to a thorn again. The moment she picked it up, it jerked in her hand, then pointed upward.

The lumpy mounds in Panjibarrh were called hills, and most of them were. Except for one. A tall shelf of dusty red stone, a ragged crag, overhung the tiny village.

On every previous visit to Panjibarrh, Eric had always thought the giant summit a comforting, sheltering rock. Not this time. The crag now looked ominous and almost frightening.

"My Portal is up there!" said Salamandra.

"And the Oobja are under the hills," said Julie, her eyes closed tightly. "I'm sensing a system of passages running beneath the ground. They are hiding there. I hear them!"

Salamandra stepped away from the others. "My way goes on alone. The little folk will tell you where Ko is. I'll find my Portal of Ages. You find Ko. Together we'll send the beast emperor away for good!"

As Salamandra and her starfox strode away through the foothills, the friends searched for and found a small opening in the earth.

Led by Julie's sense of where the hill dwellers were, the little band crawled deeper and deeper under the crag. At last, they found the hiding place of Batamogi and his people.

The moment the Oobja king saw his friends in the passageway, he jumped for joy. "Oh, my, my! Our heroes! You have come at our moment of greatest need!"

"Why are you all hiding?" asked Keeah.

The king drew his brother kings around him. "We were touring our kingdom as usual," he began. "We felt the hills shake as if something terrible was happening on the highest peak. An evil invader has come to our peaceful hills. We drew our people together and fled here."

"We believe Ko is planning a terrible attack on Jaffa City," said Keeah. "From what you have told us, he may be right above us, amassing his beasts."

"We call the summit of the Dust Hills the crown," said one of Batamogi's brothers, who introduced himself as Magibota. "Since that is where we were all crowned."

"All right, then," said Galen. "All clues point up. We must get up that mountain to its crown. And we'll need your help."

"A dusty dust storm!" said Tigomaba, another of Batamogi's brothers. "Gabitamo and I shall turn the storm wheel!"

"We shall help, too," said Mibotaga and Tomigaba in unison. "The storm we make will carry you to the top in a flash!"

"Awesome!" said Julie. "Thank you!"

"It is our pleasure!" said the kings, linking arms and bowing together.

The whole journey took no more than a few minutes. The six friends — Galen, Max, Keeah, Julie, Neal, and Eric — mounted the great wooden storm wheel in the center of the Oobja village and braced themselves.

At Batamogi's signal, the kings and the people turned the storm wheel faster and faster.

"And — up — you — go!" called Batamogi.

In a flash, the little band went flying in a coil of swiftly spinning dust. They zoomed straight up to the high crown of the hills.

The dust storm vanished as quickly as it arose, and the friends tumbled onto the summit.

As they jumped to their feet, they saw that like the rest of the landscape, the summit lay in darkness. But it was a darkness tinted with a bluish-red glow.

When their eyes adjusted to the strange light, what they saw shocked them into silence.

Nine

Goo-Goo-Gethwing!

Dust coiled here and there on the mountain like black water stirred by an invisible finger. The peaks jutted overhead like the jagged sides of a cracked bowl.

But it was the center of the summit that the friends could not take their eyes from, for there lay hundreds, thousands of black orbs, glowing with red and blue light.

"Guys," said Neal, "I think we've stumbled on Ko's stash of weird stone balls.

Maybe he's planning to bomb Droon with them."

Galen wobbled on his feet. "These are not stone balls, weird or otherwise," he said. "They are eggs! Why it has taken me so long to understand it, I do not know. They are moon dragon eggs! It is from one of these that the terrible Gethwing hatched so long ago. And here are thousands more!"

A shudder of movement rippled through the eggs, as if they all sought to roll toward the friends at the same time.

"My gosh!" said Keeah, stepping back. "Then that ball — that egg! — we found in Saleef was a baby moon dragon. It hatched on the Landboat and attacked us. And these are its brothers and sisters waiting to be born!"

Galen nodded grimly. "These dark, dust-filled hills are most like the gray mountains of the moon's far side. That is where moon dragons come from. This is some evil of Gethwing's, not of Ko's. Now I doubt if Ko is even here —"

At first, Eric didn't understand what was going on. He was drowning in a haze of confusion and anger. "Did Salamandra know this?" he asked. "How could she not know?"

A blast of lightning crashed overhead.

All of a sudden, the great dragon himself crossed in front of the moon. Gethwing alighted on a tall crag, his black shape hovering over them, larger than ever. "And I was going to surprise you, too!" he howled. "Ah, well. Maybe next time. Oh, wait. There won't be a next time!"

"Gethwing, you fiend!" cried Keeah.

"Fiend, schmiend!" snarled the moon dragon. "Arise, my sons! Arise! Seek the darkness of your calling. Come, my sons, my army, my future, my throne!"

A ripple of movement stirred the black eggs, and they began to wobble. One egg cracked, and a terrifying shriek burst out from within. The tip of a scaly black wing jerked into the air. Another cry, another wing tip. Another. Another. Another.

"Arise!" Gethwing howled.

As the friends watched, too astonished to move, the creatures emerged from their shells. They lifted into the sky in a mass of thwacking wings. Together, the dragons let out an ear-piercing shriek — *eeeeeee!* — and their cry rocked the mountains.

To Gethwing, the terrifying sound was music. "Arise, my winged sons of the moon! Arise!"

"I don't think so," said Galen. "These beasts are born and shall perish in a single moment!" In one hand he held his staff

high, while his other hand, sparking and sizzling with power, was aimed at the moon dragon.

"Yeah," said Neal, jamming his turban low. "Prepare to become egg salad, you creepies!"

"Save your silly talk for someone who cares," said Gethwing. "We're simple folk. All we really want to do is . . . *attack!*"

With astounding speed, Gethwing launched himself at the children, letting loose a firestorm upon them.

Galen fired. Keeah fired. Julie and Neal flew around as quickly as possible, hurling stones at the diving dragons. While Max spun a stout web and threw it at the attackers, Eric cast about for some kind of weapon, then skittered for cover when a dragon swooped at him.

A half-dozen beasts dived at Neal. He

floated up swiftly, but more were waiting for him and tossed him to the ground.

Julie flew at two dragons, hurtling stones at them, while Keeah blasted three others who swooped at her from behind.

Galen threw bolts of sizzling fire at Gethwing, but the dragon absorbed each shot in his clawed hands until they formed a huge single fireball. He heaved it back.

In the explosion, Galen was thrown one way, and his staff skidded across the crag in the other direction. Max darted through the rocks and ran breathlessly for the staff.

Eric pulled Keeah to safety behind a boulder. Her fingers were raw from fighting.

"This is impossible!" she cried. "Where is Salamandra?"

"No kidding!" said Neal, crawling to them, holding his shoulder in pain. "Why is she taking so long with the Portal?"

Julie cupped her ear, then turned her head. "She's coming. There!"

All at once, Salamandra, Queen of Shadowthorn, rose up above the highest peak. A ring of thorns, a hundred feet from rim to rim, spun like a hurricane behind her. The great, moving, jet-black wheel nearly blocked out the entire sky.

"Hi, everyone!" she said. "Look what I brought!"

Ten

Eric, Plain and . . . Tall

"Dragons, behind me!" Gethwing yelled. The army of newborn dragons pulled back behind their master, hovering in a moving mass of black wings.

"Salamandra, send the dragon to the past!" Galen called out as he stepped forward, Max trembling at his side. "Send his dark sons with him. Send them away — now!"

For a moment, a brief moment, all was

still on the mountaintop. Gethwing stared icily at Salamandra and she at him. Eric felt his heart racing. With a flick of her thorn staff, Salamandra could draw even the powerful Gethwing into the Portal and suck the dragons away in time, never to return.

Then Gethwing spoke.

"Sister," he said. "What took you so long?"

A cold wave of despair washed over Eric. "What?" he said softly. "What?"

Everyone turned to the queen of thorns.

Her lips, as cold and dark as ever, curved into a cruel smile. "Sorry, Gethie! Better late than never!"

"What?" cried Eric. "Salamandra? How could you? You . . . tricked us?"

"Salamandra tricked *everyone*!" said

Gethwing, laughing icily. "It was never Ko who was up here! It was never *Ko* you were following. While you have been joy-riding in your rolling thorn boat, my trap has been closing around you. And as for Ko, well, she's deceived him, too, by join-ing together with me. Poor Ko doesn't even know. Look."

They looked. And Julie screamed, "No!"

On the distant plains below, a terrible finger of fire crawled toward Jaffa City.

Ko's armies stormed across Droon, marching, marching, unstopping, unstop-pable. And visible at its head were the twin spouts of green flame Eric knew so well, leading the beasts right to the great walls of the capital.

"Ko?" cried Max. "It's Ko! Attacking Jaffa City!"

Gethwing snickered. "I told him I

would distract you, and I have. But now Salamandra and I will wait until he has fought King Zello and demolished the city, then attack him!"

"No!" cried Keeah. "My city! Jaffa City!"

"Ko isn't good for much," said Gethwing. "But he does know how to destroy. Soon your city will be ablaze! His army will be spent, and I will rule. Clever plan, no? My sons!" he cried out. "Wait for me in the pink mountains. We attack from there!"

The young moon dragons flew up and away, a black swarm of thundering wings.

Even before the dragons had faded from view, Keeah shot a stream of sparks at Gethwing, but Salamandra caught the blast in her staff. It fizzled and faded.

Galen hurled a gigantic thunderbolt at

the dragon, but the thorn queen thrust out her staff and absorbed it the same way.

"Salamandra!" cried the wizard. "You traitor! You betrayed us. You —"

"Oh, get over it, old man!" snarled the queen. "You said yourself that I work only for myself. Go and protect your tower. I imagine Ko wants to toss a torch on that himself!"

With that, she blew Galen and Max right off the mountaintop. They fell through the air until a dust storm from Batamogi sent them aloft again. Galen quickly produced the flying carpet and he and Max leaped onto it. But every time they approached her, Salamandra whirled her staff, and the Portal of Ages spun faster.

The children were awestruck. In the coiling funnel of air they saw giant masses of land, mountains, deserts — whole continents crashing toward, then away from one another. A sea of fire drowned them completely. Then came snow, then rain and forests and animals. Dwellings came next — caves at first, then desert huts, then pyramids, then palaces. Fire swept over everything, to the sound of wings flapping. The whole history of the world spun around in the roaring wind.

Eric read Salamandra's eyes. He saw what Gethwing saw. That the future belonged to the moon dragon.

It was *his*.

In that moment, he tried to remember what had first brought Salamandra to Droon. Had he and his friends really forced her to flee to Droon?

Or was there another reason she was here? A reason buried in the mists of past time that only she knew? Or a reason waiting to be discovered in some unknown future?

Before he could move, before anyone could move, Salamandra pointed her staff at the four children. They were dragged across the mountaintop toward Gethwing.

"No!" shouted Keeah. "Stop this —"

Gethwing grabbed Julie as if she were no more than a feather. Smiling cruelly, he tossed her toward the spinning Portal.

Julie cried out for a second, then disappeared into the roaring wind.

Neal shrieked, "Oh, my —"

Laughing, Gethwing snatched Neal next and threw him over his massive shoulders and right into the Portal. Neal was gone, too. Then the moon dragon turned to Keeah, who was blasting with all her might, and heaved her into the spinning funnel.

"Keeah!" Eric yelled, flailing his arms to reach her, but she was sucked into the dark hurricane like the others.

Gethwing leaped to the ground next to

Eric. His face wore a stone-cold expression of hatred. "You, boy, will be lost in the past now. Not me. You will suffer. Not me. You will never rule Droon. I shall. Droon is mine —"

"But the boy is mine!" said Salamandra. She aimed her staff at Eric, and he was pulled across the ground to her feet.

"Salamandra!" Eric screamed over the Portal's roaring winds. "Why are you doing this?"

She stared at him, her eyes flashing. Then she thrust her staff at him as if to pick him up and toss him into the Portal.

Hardly knowing what he was doing, Eric grabbed the clump of thorns at the staff's head with both hands to keep it from striking him. The sharp thorns cut into his flesh. They stung him. He nearly cried out. But the moment he grabbed the staff, his mind exploded with an image.

The image of an apple tree.

It was nearly fruitless, its branches bare and black. All around the tree it was late autumn, nearly winter, but still warm.

A small boy — Eric knew at once it was himself — sat on a branch of the tree. His face was turned away, watching a man approach him slowly.

The man was old, frail, white-haired, white-faced. "Eric . . ." the man said, "we're together again . . . let me help you. . . ."

The man reached out his hand, withered and white. When Eric touched it with his own, the branches around him turned silver as if moonlight had splashed down suddenly.

Eric knew as sure as anything that this was no vision. It was a memory from his youth.

When the image faded, Eric turned his eyes to Salamandra.

What does this mean? he asked silently, knowing that only by holding the thorn staff did he have the power to speak so.

Reki-ur-set, the thorn queen responded.

Eric frowned. *I don't know languages — You should. It is your own.*

"Sister Salamandra," said Gethwing. "Enough of this silent staring. If you can't get rid of him fast, I shall. We have business to do. We have a pact. Good-bye forever, Eric Hinkle!"

Gethwing pushed Eric toward the portal. The force of the wind was staggering. Eric's feet left the ground and dangled into the funnel. The only thing keeping him on the mountaintop was his grip on the thorn staff.

Feeling his strength leave him, he stared at Salamandra one last time. He saw in her eyes one thing only. And he heard in his mind four simple words.

You can do it!

Eric looked at his helpless fingers and realized that they were no more helpless than anyone else's. He could still open closets. He could still lift veils away and see what lay behind them. He could help his friends up when they fell. If he couldn't understand languages, he could still understand his own. If he didn't have visions, he still had vision.

It didn't matter if he was as ordinary, as normal, or as plain as anyone else. Because like anyone, he could think and feel and say what he believed.

And he could do something about it.

"Good-bye, former wizard!" Gethwing bellowed with laughter. He began to pry the boy's hands loose from the staff.

"Good-bye, yourself!" Eric said. "And wizard or not, I'm still Eric Hinkle! You'll never conquer Droon as long as I'm around —"

Releasing one hand from the jagged thorns, Eric reached out and clutched Gethwing by the neck. Then he pulled the moon dragon as hard as he could.

Gethwing stumbled on his feet, howling in surprise, but he could not fly against the wind. The Portal swept around him, and he was sucked, wailing, into the depths of time.

Gethwing was gone.

The thorns piercing his fingers sent pain shooting through Eric's body. "Salamandra, help me! Return my powers!" he cried.

The queen's eyes flashed and were suddenly wet with tears. Then, as she jerked her staff away from him, she said, "Remember, Eric. Remember. *Reki-ur-set!*"

Eric couldn't take the pain any longer.

The thorns slipped away, and so did he. The last thing he saw before the Portal closed over him was Galen and Max flying toward the flaming storm on the plains below.

"Droon!" he cried out. "Drooooooon!"

Then his eyes closed, he fell away, and all was darkness.